MW01121401

Dedicated to:
My family, friends, and teachers, and to all
the circus animals and performers who have
brought us leaping lions, awesome acrobats,
excitement and exhilaration, and most of all,
the laughter that brings us together.

COPYRIGHT © 1996 BY LINDSEY WOLTER

International Standard Book Number: 0-933849-61-3 (LIB.BDG.)

Library of Congress Cataloging-in-Publication Data
Wolter, Lindsey, 1986-
    Circus adventures / written and illustrated by Lindsey Wolter.
    p.   cm.
    Summary: While at the circus, a girl suddenly becomes part
of the show after being swooped up by the lady on the horse.
ISBN 0-933849-61-3 (lib.bdg. : alk. paper)
 1. Children's writings, American.
[1. Circus—Fiction.
 2. Children's writings.   3. Children's art.]

I. Title.
PZ7.W8367Ci   1996
[E]—dc20   96-11421
                               CIP
                               AC

Creative Coordinator: David Melton
Editorial Coordinator: Nancy R. Thatch
Production Assistant: Brian Hubbard

Printed in the United States of America

Landmark Editions, Inc.
P.O. Box 270169
1402 Kansas Avenue
Kansas City, Missouri 64127
(816) 241-4919

CIRCUS ADVENTURES

This book is loaded with action! Molly, the central character, goes to the circus, and before she knows it, she becomes one of the performers. And there she goes! Molly is tossed and she is thrown. She is flipped and she is flung. She is grabbed and she is dropped. She's even shot from a cannon. But somehow she always lands on her feet or on her seat, then gets right up and is propelled into her next adventure.

Lindsey Wolter is to be commended for her skills as a writer. Her text is exactly as it should be in a picture-story book. It is quick, to the point, and never slows down the action.

At first glance, one might think Lindsey's illustrations are simple, but they aren't. Her drawings appear simple only because they were so well-planned and composed. The actions of the characters throughout the book were choreographed as precisely as a ballet by Balanchine or a dance routine by Bob Fosse.

The costumes, scenery, and stunts didn't just happen either. Lindsey designed all the costumes and all the sets. She also created and directed all the dangerous action sequences. She assures me that Molly herself performed all of her own stunts and never once used a double.

Lindsey was an absolute joy to work with! She was full of ideas, she listened carefully to instructions, and she worked with the speed of summer lightning. Editor Nan Thatch and I loved watching her create this sensational book!

So — Come one! Come all! Welcome to the Big Top! The fun is about to begin!

—David Melton
Creative Coordinator
Landmark Editions, Inc.

CIRCUS ADVENTURES

written and illustrated by

LINDSEY WOLTER

LANDMARK EDITIONS, INC

P.O. Box 270169 1402 Kansas Avenue   Kansas City, Missouri 64127
(816) 241-4919

My name is Molly. Last week my mother took me to the circus. We sat in seats on the very front row.

I was so excited! I could hardly wait for the big show to begin.

6

Suddenly a whistle blew and the band started to play.
Then the bright spotlights came on.

Circus performers paraded into the tent. A beautiful
lady on a white horse led the way.

Then something happened that really surprised me.
The lady stopped her horse right in front of me.

"Would you like to take a ride?" she asked.

"Oh, yes!" I replied. And I climbed onto the horse's
back and waved to my mother.

I felt very important as we rode around the track. But then the horse started to gallop faster and faster. I bounced up and down and finally slid off of its back.

Just in time I grabbed hold of the horse's tail. I held on as tight as I could, but not for long. I lost my grip and . . .

. . . landed in the clowns' dressing room!

"Hurry up and get ready!" one of the clowns told me.

"It's almost time for our act to begin."

10

Before I could say anything, the clowns dressed me in
a funny costume. They slipped big shoes on my feet and put
a bright red nose on my face.

Then we jumped onto the clowns' fire truck.

The siren blared as we drove into the tent. The crowd cheered while we sped around and around the track.

Suddenly the fire truck stopped. All of the clowns got

out and started throwing pies at each other.

Before one of the pies could hit me, a big gray snake slithered in. It wrapped itself around my waist and pulled me away from the clowns. But guess what . . .

. . . It wasn't a slithery snake.

It was an elephant's trunk!

The elephant was very friendly. She lifted me up and set me down on her back. What fun!

Everything was going just fine until a mouse scurried across the floor.

The elephant was so frightened, she screamed and reared up on her hind legs! And I was thrown . . .

15

. . . into a lion's cage!

The lion got very angry. He opened his mouth wide and roared. He had the biggest, sharpest teeth I had ever seen. I was really scared!

16

The ferocious lion roared again and started toward me.

I picked up a chair and grabbed a whip.

CRACK! I snapped the whip at him.

Then I opened the cage door, ran outside, and . . .

. . . I started climbing up the first thing I came to —

a human pyramid of acrobats!

"Stop that!" the acrobats screamed at me. "You'll

knock us over!"

But I didn't stop. I kept on climbing.

That made the acrobats lose their balance. And down
we tumbled.

Everyone hit the ground, except me. I dropped . . .

. . . onto the handlebars of a bear's bicycle!

The bear was so surprised, he didn't even growl at me.

And he forgot to watch where he was going.

"Look out!" I yelled.

But my warning was too late.

The bear crashed his bicycle into the popcorn machine!
Popcorn exploded everywhere. The bear rolled across the
floor. And I was flipped head–over–heels into . . .

. . . a cannon!

It was dark inside the cannon. And I was stuck! Will I ever get out of here? I wondered.

Then I heard a strange sound. *HSSSSSSSSS!*

BOOM!!!

Like a rocket, I was shot into the air!

UP, UP, UP, I went! HIGHER and HIGHER I soared!

But just before I hit the top of the tent . . .

. . . two hands grabbed hold of mine!

It was the man on the flying trapeze. High above the
ground, he swung me back and forth.

"Are you ready to do our big trick?" he asked.

"What big trick?" I replied.

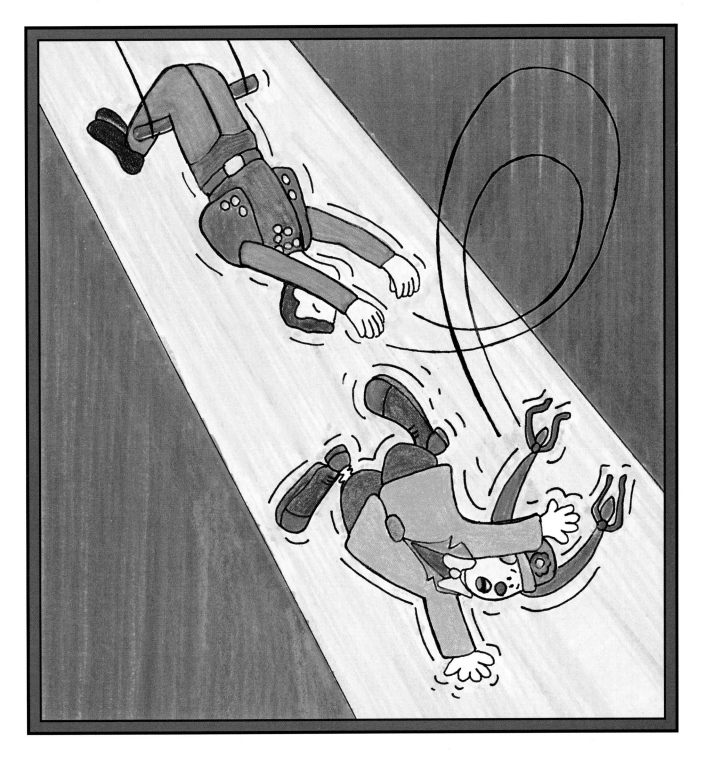

"This big trick," he said as he let go of my hands.

And I went flying loop–the–loop through the air!

The crowd loved it! They clapped and cheered.

Then I began to fall — DOWN! DOWN! DOWN!

toward the ground below . . .

. . . But I didn't hit the ground. I fell into a net!

That net was so bouncy, it bounced me back up into the air. And I landed *KERPLUNK* in the seat right next to my mother.

26

"Molly!" she exclaimed. "Where have you been? And what is that red thing on your face?"

"Mom," I said, "you will never believe what happened to me."

Next week my dad is going to take me to see the big
parade. But this time, I will not get into any trouble,
because this time, I won't be on the very front row.

This time I am going to stand way back in the middle
of the crowd and *just watch!*

"HELP!"

BOOKS FOR STUDENTS
– WINNERS OF THE NATIONAL WRITTEN &

Karen Kerber
age 12

David McAdoo
age 14

Amy Hagstrom
age 9

Isaac Whitlatch
age 11

Michael Cain
age 11

Amity Gaige
age 16

Adam Moore
age 9

Ben Kendall
age 7

Steven Shepard
age 13

Travis Williams
age 16

by Karen Kerber, age 12
St. Louis, Missouri
A delightfully playful book! The text is loaded with clever alliterations and gentle humor. Karen's brightly colored illustrations are composed of wiggly and waggly strokes of genius.
Printed Full Color
ISBN 0-933849-29-X

by David McAdoo, age 14
Springfield, Missouri
An exciting intergalactic adventure! In the distant future, a courageous warrior defends a kingdom from an invading dragon from outer space. Astounding sepia illustrations.
Printed Duotone
ISBN 0-933849-23-0

by Amy Hagstrom, age 9
Portola, California
An exciting western! When a boy and an old Indian try to save a herd of wild ponies, they discover a lost canyon and see the mystical vision of the Great White Stallion.
Printed Full Color
ISBN 0-933849-15-X

by Isaac Whitlatch, age 11
Casper, Wyoming
The true confessions of a devout vegetable hater! Isaac tells ways to avoid and dispose of the "slimy green things." His colorful illustrations provide a salad of laughter and mirth.
Printed Full Color
ISBN 0-933849-16-8

by Michael Cain, age 11
Annapolis, Maryland
A glorious tale of adventure! To become a knight, a young man must face a beast in the forest, a spellbinding witch, and a giant bird that guards a magic oval crystal.
Printed Full Color
ISBN 0-933849-26-5

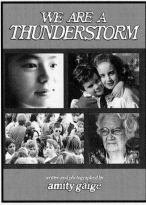

by Amity Gaige, age 16
Reading, Pennsylvania
A lyrical blend of poetry and photographs! Amity's sensitive poems offer thought-provoking ideas and amusing insights. This lovely book is one to be savored and enjoyed.
Printed Full Color
ISBN 0-933849-27-3

by Adam Moore, age 9
Broken Arrow, Oklahoma
A remarkable true story! When Adam was eight years old, he fell and ran an arrow into his head. With rare insight and humor, he tells of his ordeal and his amazing recovery.
Printed Two Colors
ISBN 0-933849-24-9

by Michael Aushenker, age 19
Ithaca, New York
Chomp! Chomp! When Arthur gets to feed his goat, the animal everything in sight. A very story – good to the last bite illustrations are terrific.
Printed Full Color
ISBN 0-933849-28-1

SPECIAL NOTICE!

Your students will want to see and read all of the BOOKS FOR STUDENTS BY STUDENTS!® These wonderful books entertain, motivate and inspire!

"After I showed the WINNING BOOKS to my students," says Rhonda Freese, Teacher, "all they wanted to do was WRITE! WRITE! WRITE! and DRAW! DRAW! DRAW!

Now the BOOKS FOR STUDENTS BY STUDENTS!® are included in:

the Accelerated Reader ™
Computer Reading Management System
Disk I.D.: E-34

by Benjamin Kendall, age 7
State College, Pennsylvania
When Ben wears his new super-hero costume, he sees Aliens who are from outer space. His attempts to stop the pesky invaders provide loads of laughs. Colorful drawings add to the fun!
Printed Full Color
ISBN 0-933849-42-7

by Steven Shepard, age 13
Great Falls, Virginia
A gripping thriller! When a boy rows his boat to an island to retrieve a stolen knife, he faces threatening fog, treacherous currents, and a sinister lobsterman. Outstanding drawings!
Printed Full Color
ISBN 0-933849-43-5

by Travis Williams, age 16
Sardis, B.C., Canada
A chilling mystery! When a boy discovers his classmates a ing, he becomes entrapped in conflicting stories, false alibis, a ening changes. Dramatic drawi
Printed Two Color
ISBN 0-933849-44-3

These Books Motivate and Inspire Readers! **ORDER TODA**

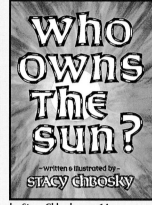

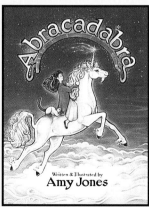

Leslie A MacKeen
age 9

Elizabeth Haidle
age 13

Heidi Salter
age 19

Lauren Peters
age 7

Jayna Miller
age 19

Alise Leggat
age 8

Lisa Butenhoff
age 13

Shintaro Maeda
age 8

Miles MacGregor
age 12

Kristin Pedersen
age 18

by Leslie Ann MacKeen, age 9
Winston-Salem, North Carolina
Loaded with fun and puns! When Jeremiah T. Fitz's car stops running, several animals offer suggestions for fixing it. The results are hilarious. The illustrations are charming.
Printed Full Color
ISBN 0-933849-19-2

by Elizabeth Haidle, age 13
Beaverton, Oregon
A very touching story! The grumpiest Elfkin learns to cherish the friendship of others after he helps an injured snail and befriends an orphaned boy. Absolutely beautiful.
Printed Full Color
ISBN 0-933849-20-6

by Heidi Salter, age 19
Berkeley, California
Spooky and wonderful! To save her vivid imagination, a young girl must confront the Great Grey Grimly himself. The narrative is filled with suspense. Vibrant illustrations.
Printed Full Color
ISBN 0-933849-21-4

by Lauren Peters, age 7
Kansas City, Missouri
The Christmas that almost was When Santa Claus takes a vaca Mrs. Claus and the elves go strike. Toys aren't made. Coo aren't baked. Super illustrations.
Printed Full Color
ISBN 0-933849-25-7

by Jayna Miller, age 19
Zanesville, Ohio
The funniest Halloween ever! When Jammer the Rabbit takes all the treats, his friends get even. Their hilarious scheme includes a haunted house and mounds of chocolate.
Printed Full Color
ISBN 0-933849-37-0

by Alise Leggat, age 8
Culpepper, Virginia
Amy J. Kendrick wants to play football, but her mother wants her to become a ballerina. Their clash of wills creates hilarious situations. Clever, delightful illustrations.
Printed Full Color
ISBN 0-933849-39-7

by Lisa Kirsten Butenhoff, age 13
Woodbury, Minnesota
The people of a Russian Village face the winter without warm clothes or enough food. Then their lives are improved by a young girl's gifts. A tender story with lovely illustrations.
Printed Full Color
ISBN 0-933849-40-0

by Jennifer Brady, age 17
Columbia, Missouri
When poachers capture a pri lions, a native boy tries to fre animals. A skillfully told Glowing illustrations illumina African adventure.
Printed Full Color
ISBN 0-933849-41-9

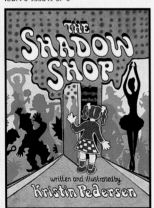

by Kristin Pedersen, age 18
Etobicoke, Ont., Canada
A mysterious parable, told in rhyme. When Thelma McMurty trades her shadow, she thinks she will live happily ever after. But an old gypsy knows better. The collage illustrations are brilliant!
Printed Full Color
ISBN 0-933849-53-2

by Laura Hughes, age 8
Woonsocket, Rhode Island
When a Dakota Indian girl finds a herd of buffalo, the big hunt of the year begins! An exciting fiction-based-on-fact story with wonderful illustrations that younger children will enjoy.
Printed Full Color
ISBN 0-933849-57-5

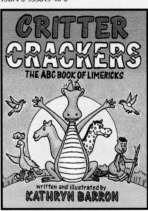

by Kathryn Barron, age 13
Emo, Ont., Canada
Funny from A to Z! Kathryn's hilarious limericks and delightfully witty illustrations provide laughs, page after page! An absolutely charming book for young children.
Printed Full Color
ISBN 0-933849-58-3

by Taramesha Maniatty, age
Morrisville, Vermont
A young man is determined dog-sledding team will win the during the competition, he is f make the most difficult decisio life. Brilliant text and paintings.
Printed Full Color
ISBN 0-933849-59-1